D0230214

Llyfrgelloedd Caerdydd
www.cardydd.gov.uk/llyfrgelloedd
Cardiff Libraries
www.cardiff.gov.uk/libraries

CAERDYDD
CARDIFF

ACC. No: 07053737

First published in the UK in 2019
by New Frontier Publishing Europe Ltd
93 Harbord Street, London SW6 6PN
www.newfrontierpublishing.co.uk

ISBN: 978-1-912076-37-6

Text copyright © 2019 Lana Spasevski
Illustrations copyright © 2019 Penelope Pratley
The rights of Lana Spasevski to be identified as the author and
Penelope Pratley to be identified as the illustrator of this work have been asserted.

All rights reserved.

This book is sold subject to the condition that it shall not, by way of trade or otherwise, be lent,
hired out or otherwise circulated in any form of binding or cover other than that in which it is published.
No part of this publication may be reproduced, stored in a retrieval system, or transmitted,
in any form or by any means (electronic, mechanical, photocopying, recording or otherwise),
without the prior written permission of New Frontier Publishing (Europe) Pty. Ltd.

A CIP catalogue record for this book
is available from the British Library.

Designed by Verity Clark

Printed in China
10 9 8 7 6 5 4 3 2 1

Max's Dinosaur Feet!

For my dearest daughters
Alessia and Elina.

~ L S

For James and Beth
With special thanks to my family.

~ P P

Max's Dinosaur Feet!

Lana Spasevski

Penelope Pratley

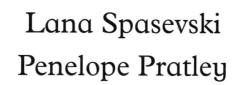

Max has **dinosaur** feet.

SToMp!

StaMp!

SMAsh!

'Dinosaur stampede!' roars Max.

'Shhh, you'll wake Molly,' whispers Mum. 'Walk softly, Dinosaur Max,' she adds.

Max looks at his dinosaur feet. 'How?' he asks.

'Walk on dinosaur eggshells.
But make sure they don't crack!'
says Mum, and winks.
Max and Mum practise walking on
dinosaur eggshells. Tiptoe,
tiptoe . . .

All is quiet.

Max's dinosaur feet
won't wake Molly now.

But Dad's happy summer
feet will.

Drip!

SliP!

'Follow us, Dad.
We'll show you how
to walk on dinosaur
eggshells.'

Tiptoe,

tiptoe . . .

All is quiet again.

But not for long.

It's Pop with his
new walking feet.

ThUd!

THuMp!

THwAck!

'Shhh, you'll wake
Molly!' squeals Max.

'Follow us, Pop. We'll show you how to walk on dinosaur eggshells.'

Tiptoe,

tiptoe . . .

All is quiet again.

But then Merida prances in
with her dazzling dancing feet.

SwAy!

'Shhh, you'll wake
Molly!' cries Max.

'Follow us, Merida. We'll show you how to walk on dinosaur eggshells.'

Tiptoe,

tiptoe . . .

Finally, all is quiet.

But then Rufus charges in.
He has a wrinkly wet nose
that just loves feet!

Sniff!

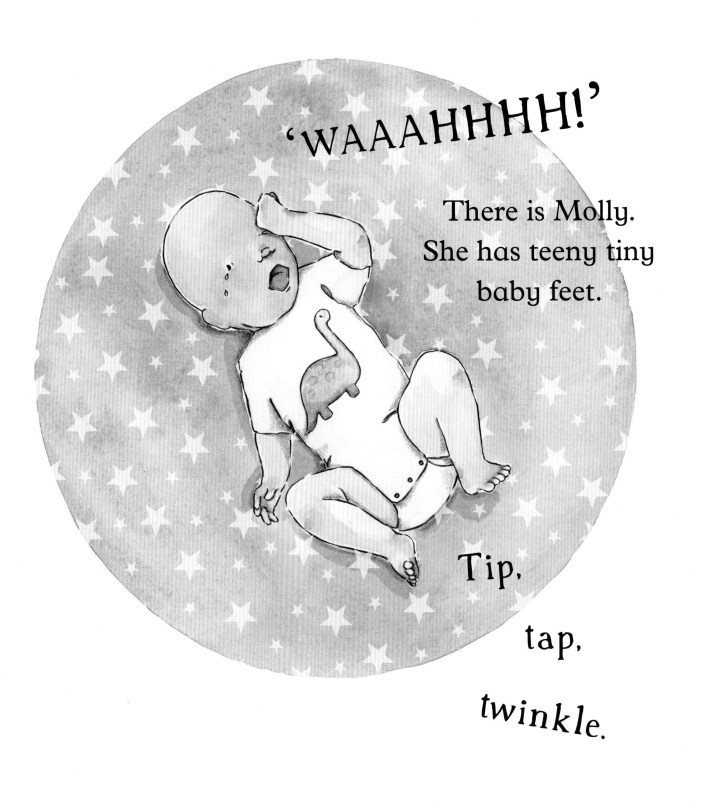

'WAAAHHHH!'

There is Molly.
She has teeny tiny
baby feet.

Tip,

tap,

twinkle.

'I'm sorry our noisy feet woke you, Dinosaur Molly,' says Max.

'Close your eyes. I'll tell you a story,' he whispers.

'Once upon a time,
there were five little dinosaurs.

This little dinosaur went to the forest,
This little dinosaur stayed home.
This little dinosaur had roasted leaves for dinner,
And this little dinosaur had none.'

'This little dinosaur got very, very sleepy
and yawned all the way home.'

Tiptoe,

tiptoe . . .

All is quiet again.

For now . . .